Mountains of the Moon
Valley of the Shadow
River of the Rainbow
Vilcabamba

THE FIRST STORY EVER TOLD

BY Erik Jendresen
AND Alberto Villoldo
ILLUSTRATED BY Yoshi

Simon & Schuster Books for Young Readers

AUTHOR'S NOTE

The First Story Ever Told was inspired by the creation tales of the Incas of Peru. The name Inca means "Child of the Sun." Before they were conquered by a Spanish invasion in the 16th century, the Incas built one of the greatest empires the world has ever seen. They cultivated over one hundred food products, including the potato; established a social security system; and engineered great cities connected by tunnels, suspension bridges, and thousands of miles of paved roads. They charted the course of the sun and the moon and they believed that the sun was their father and the Earth was their mother and that gold was "the tears wept by the Sun." They left behind no written history, but a vivid tradition. It is a privilege to find the words for *The First Story Ever Told* and a joy to see such a love story captured by Yoshi's expert brushwork.

SIMON & SCHUSTER BOOKS FOR YOUNG READERS
An imprint of Simon & Schuster Children's Publishing Division, 1230 Avenue of the Americas, New York, New York 10020
Text copyright © 1996 by Erik Jendresen and Alberto Villoldo. Illustrations copyright © 1996 by Yoshi.
SIMON & SCHUSTER BOOKS FOR YOUNG READERS is a trademark of Simon & Schuster.
Book design by Paul Zakris. The text for this book is set in 16-point Centaur.
The illustrations are rendered in watercolor.
Printed and bound in the United States of America
First Edition
10 9 8 7 6 5 4 3 2 1
Library of Congress Cataloging-in-Publication Data
Jendresen, Erik.
The first story ever told / by Erik Jendresen and Alberto Villoldo : illustrated by Yoshi.
p.   cm.
Summary: An explorer goes in search of the Inca's legendary lost city of gold, but discovers instead a more spiritual treasure.
[1. Creation—Fiction. 2. Explorers—Fiction. 3. Peru—Fiction. 4. Incas—Fiction.
5. Indians of South America—Fiction.] I. Yoshi, ill. II. Title.
PZ7.V73Fi 1996
[E]—dc20   95-6062
ISBN 0-689-80515-2

For Savannah Aslee Bobis,
Ian Pedro and Alexis Robyn McCulloch-Villoldo,
children of the Sun.
—E. J.

To my son, Ian, and our dreams and adventures.
—A. V.

To Hibiki Miyazaki and Joan Wilcox, with thanks and
appreciation for their help in bringing this story to life.
—Y.

There was once an explorer who traveled many miles over land and by sea, up mountains and across deserts. And every place he went he heard the legend of Vilcabamba, a City of Gold that was hidden in the jungle.

One day he went to a museum where he found a display of ancient gold objects. In the bottom of a glass case there was a map drawn on a piece of paper that was as dry and cracked as an old brown leaf. It was hard to read because the writing was faded and the paper was stained.

The map showed the way to the lost City of Gold.

The explorer wasted no time. He packed his bags and followed the directions on the map.

He sailed across the sea to find the Mountains of the Moon. He hiked a trail past great boulders all the way to the highest peak.

And when he had climbed the Mountains of the Moon, he descended a jagged rock trail down into the Valley of the Shadow.

There were people in the valley who had heard the legend of Vilcabamba, but no one knew where it could be found. So the explorer pushed on.

By the time he came to the River of the Rainbow he was very tired. He stopped and drank from the water rippling over the smooth round stones in the river bed. The map showed he had only to follow the river into the jungle to find Vilcabamba.

But the sun had set and there was darkness all around. The jungle was wet and green, and there were trees with thick trunks and plants with huge leaves and vines that wrapped themselves around everything. And there were sounds in the jungle—parrots squawking, monkeys screeching, jaguars growling, and great snakes slithering.

The explorer knew that he could go no farther that night. So he built a fire inside a circle of stones. And as he gazed into the firelight he thought he could see walls of gold glistening in the flames and rising into the smoke. But he was tired and knew it was time to sleep.

He rested his head on his arm and closed
his eyes.

And he dreamed.

The jungle grew quiet and the hiss of the fire
became the whispering voice of a very
old woman.

"I am Grandmother Fire," she said. "Listen,
and I will tell you the first story ever told.

"The story begins," she whispered, "before there were plants, before there were animals. There were only the mountains and the valleys and the great oceans.

"The Earth was a young maiden. The Moon was her sister. The Sun was the brightest star in the heavens. And the Earth loved the Sun. She danced around the great star, spinning all the while to show off her beauty. And while the Earth danced, the Moon watched over her.

"Sister Moon also loved the Sun. But when she saw the Sun beam upon the Earth, she began hiding her face in shadow.

"One night, when the face of the Moon was turned away, the Sun and the Earth confessed their love for each other.

"And the Sun shed a tear of joy that landed on the Earth.

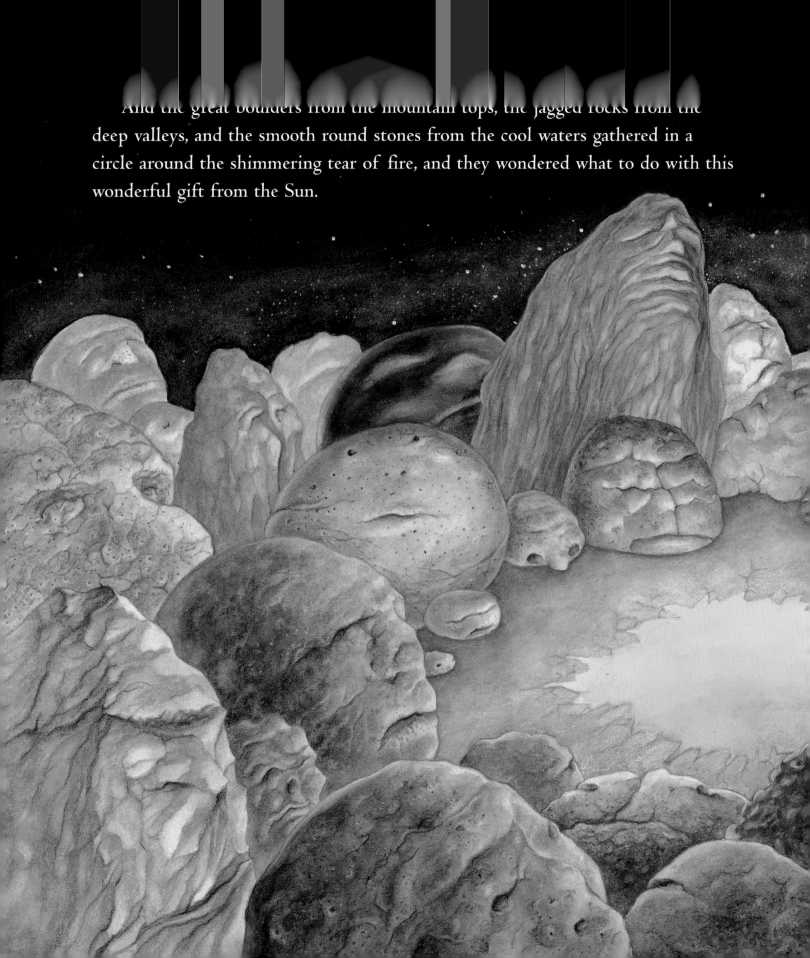

And the great boulders from the mountain tops, the jagged rocks from the deep valleys, and the smooth round stones from the cool waters gathered in a circle around the shimmering tear of fire, and they wondered what to do with this wonderful gift from the Sun.

One day a little river stone arrived at the great circle of stones. She was smooth and shiny but no bigger than the tip of your finger, and she could not see what the circle held. So, to catch a glimpse of the Sun's great gift, she jumped with all her power. When she finally jumped high enough to see the tear of fire, she had an idea.

"'I know what to do!' she cried. 'We must take this gift to the center of the Earth, to the place where we were born! Do as I do! Jump!'

"So the Stone People began to jump. The circle was broken, and the tear of fire began to spread to the four corners of the Earth. But as the Stone People jumped, the ground trembled, cracked, and opened. And the great tear of fire rushed like a river of gold into the crack and fell down, all the way to the heart of the Earth, where it would burn forever.

"Now you know why the Moon hides her face every month. Now you know how fire came to the Earth, and why we build a circle of stones around our campfires. And you know how Father Sun's love burns deep within the heart of Mother Earth.

"But there is more. . . .

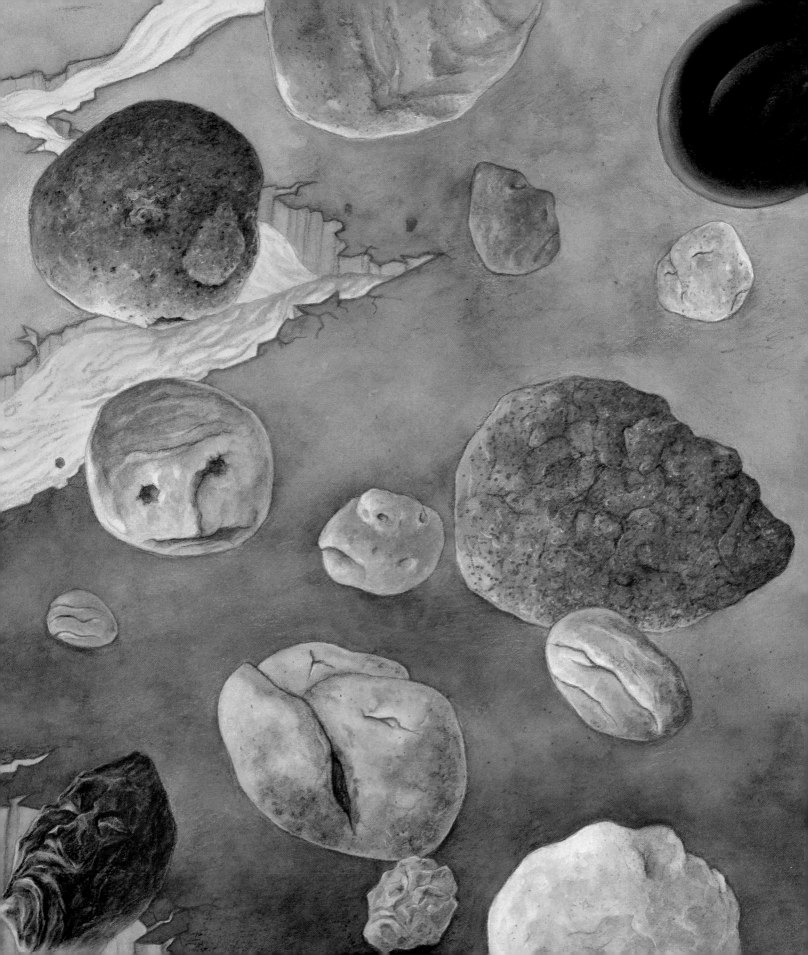

"When the Sun's fire reached the center of the Earth, life was born. The waters of the Earth were warmed and soon the Plant People and the Animal People were born from the Earth's ocean womb. Then the Children of the Sun emerged from the sea at the top of the world and joined the plants and animals and stones who lived in the forests of Mother Earth.

"And in the valleys and along the rivers where the great tear of fire had flowed and cooled, they would find something soft that shone like the Sun, and this was gold. The Children of the Sun gathered the gold from the ground and wore it close to their hearts.

"Much later, long after people had moved to the four corners of the Earth, there were some who forgot that the Earth was their mother and the Sun was their father. They came across the sea to take the gold from the Children of the Sun.

"So the Children of the Sun took what was left of the Sun's ancient gift and disappeared.

"They closed their eyes and went to a place where all they could see was gold. They heard the ancient voices telling the first story ever told, and they felt the love of Father Sun and Mother Earth. They called this place Vilcabamba, The Sacred Place.

"When the Others heard of The Sacred Place, they thought it was a great City of Gold in the jungle. They tried to follow the Children of the Sun. But they were fooled. Vilcabamba is not a city. It is not a place that you can walk to. It is the place that we find when we close our eyes and see the light of creation and hear the first story ever told. It is where you are now."

When the explorer opened his eyes it was morning.

The fire had gone out and the Old Woman was nowhere to be seen. He stood beside the circle of stones and looked at the jungle shining golden in the early morning light of the Sun.

He lifted his face, closed his eyes, and saw the light glowing through his eyelids. He felt the Sun fill his body with warmth.

And he knew that he had found Vilcabamba.